D1318134

Maureen + Ed
We hope you enjoy
our book.
Rob
(Robert Martin)
Keira

# SUPER CLARA

A Young Girl's Story of Cancer, Bravery and Courage!

## Robert Martin with Keira Ely

### Illustrations by Dave Drotleff

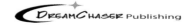

DreamChaser Publishing

SuperClara: A Young Girl's Story of Cancer, Bravery and Courage!
by Robert Martin with Keira Ely

Published by

RobertMartinAuthor.com

SuperClara: A Young Girl's Story of Cancer, Bravery and Courage!
is a registered trademark of DreamChaser Publishing LLC

Illustrations: Dave Drotleff

Book Layout: Nick Zelinger, NZ Graphics

ISBN 978-0-9908317-3-0 (Hardcover)
ISBN 978-0-9908317-4-7 (Softcover)
ISBN 978-0-9908317-5-4 (eBook)

LCCN: 2017906424

Children's, Health, Courage, Adversity, Cancer

Printed in the United States of America

First Edition

*To my granddaughter, Clara.*
*You will always be my lovely cupcake.*
*Papa*

*To my amazing sister, Clara.*
*If I had a flower for every time I thought of you,*
*I could walk through my garden forever.*
*Keira*

At least, I did until today. Today is different.
Today, I need help to fix something that is wrong.
Lately my head has been hurting a lot.
Doctor Carl says I have a lump on my brain.
He says I need to have an operation to remove it.

*I'm trying to be positive, but today ... I'm a little scared.*

When I wake up from the operation, there is
a humongous bandage on my head.
My Mom squishes my hand.

"Don't look so worried, Mom! I'm OK."
*Inside, I don't feel as positive as I sound to Mom.*

"You're right, Clara." Mom says.
"You are OK! Doctor Carl even said
you can go back to school next week!"

At school, Alicia yells, "Hooray! Clara's back!"
Steve asks, "Where did your hair go?"
"Were you sick?" asks Justin.
I pull my hat down on my head and do my best to smile.

"I had a lump removed from my head.
Doctor Carl called it cancer."
"What's cancer?" Alicia asks.

"Cancer is like a gang of bad guys. No one knows where they come from. But when they get into our body, they try and beat up the good guys that keep our bodies healthy," I reply.

"What did the cancer lump look like?" asks Justin.

"My cancer lump looked like a ball of tiny white marshmallows smashed together, with itsy bitsy specks of yucky red chili peppers stuck to it. The tiny white marshmallows are the good guys. The red chili peppers are the bad guys, the cancer. They're very mean and as they get bigger they get meaner. They hurt my head a lot."

"Wow, we think you're super brave!" says Steve.
*But I don't feel super brave.*

When I go back to see Doctor Carl, he says,
"Today, we're going to give you medicine to
make sure those bad guys don't come back."

"Why do I need medicine?"

"Clara, do you know why you go to school?" Doctor Carl asks. "Mom says that if I study, read and do my homework, it will make my brain stronger," I say. "But what does school have to do with cancer and medicine?"

"Well, medicine helps your brain get stronger too. That's how you keep the cancer bad guys away."

"How about I take the medicine for one week?" I say.
"Clara, I'm afraid that just like school, you need to
take the medicine for a long time to keep the
bad guys away."

*Why me?* I wonder. *Why did I have to get cancer?*
*Did I do something wrong?*

Mom always knows what I'm thinking.
"No one is sure why you have cancer, Clara," she says.
"But we do know that it isn't because of anything
you did, or thought, or said."

"Thank goodness!" I smile.
*But having to take medicine for that long still stinks!*

The next time I visit Dr. Carl, he says, "Clara, it's time for you to meet Mister Ray. You'll be spending time with him for the next six weeks. He has special lights to shine on your head. Their job is to chase away any bad guys that might still be hiding in there."

"No way!" I start to say, but then I am surprised by what I see. "Look, Lamby! That machine is smiling. Maybe Mister Ray is going to be a friend."

Mister Ray's shining lights begin to dance on my head.
Something good is happening. I can feel it!

When the six weeks with Mister Ray is over, I say,
"Goodbye, Mister Ray. Thanks for helping!"

On my way home from the hospital, I pass a park with squirrels, birds and chipmunks. Suddenly, I feel like I can tell how each one is feeling—the squirrel is sad, the bird is mad, and the chipmunk is scared. Just like how I felt getting my operation, taking my medicine and seeing Mr. Ray!

*Maybe Mister Ray's special lights gave me SuperClara Powers?*

I stop and sing a little song to them,
hoping they will understand what I say:
"Sad, mad or scared you don't have to be!
Smile and be happy for all to see."

What? Hey guys, she did understand what we are feeling inside!

There is something truly special about her.

They all gather around me and start
to whistle a beautiful, happy tune together.
*Wow, maybe I really do have SuperClara Powers!*

The next day, Mom and I take Maggie for a walk.
Uh-oh! There's Fang, the neighborhood bully.
Maggie breaks away from me and starts running.
Fang charges after her. What can I do?

I know! I'll use my SuperClara Power!

I sing to Maggie:
"Small and afraid you don't have to be!
Be brave and stay strong for all to see."
Maggie stops and looks Fang straight in the eyes.

They both wag their tails, and then they start
playing together! Maggie is now more like me
when it comes to something scary—brave!

Mom and Dad take me to the zoo. I love the sea lions!
But why is Fuzzy hiding? Then I notice her whiskers
are a lot shorter than the other sea lions'.

She feels like I used to—worried what my friends
might say about my hair!

I sing her a song:
"Self-conscious and worried you don't have to be!
Believe in yourself for all to see."
Fuzzy swims out to play with the other sea lions.

My SuperClara Power tells me she feels confident,
just like me—I think my hairstyle is cool now!

Next, we see my favorites—the cheetahs.
I like Dash the best. But today, Dash looks annoyed
and his roar sounds more like a whine.
The zookeeper is trying to give him some medicine.
My SuperClara Power tells me what Dash is thinking.

That's just like I used to be—whining and hiding
when it was time to take my medicine!

I sing a song to him:
"Stubborn and whiny you don't have to be!
Drink up and get well for all to see."

Dash gobbles up his medicine,
easy-peasy lemon-squeezy.

That reminds me, I have to take mine!
I've been taking my medicine for a year now.
I feel great!

Mom and Dad take me for a special dinner
to celebrate my first year of beating
the cancer bad guys.

"Mom, Dad, look!" I shout. "Doctor Carl, Maggie, Fang, Fuzzy, Dash and even Mr. Ray are here!"

"Yay! This is the best surprise, ever! I am so happy!"

"We are so proud of you, Clara," they say.
"In one year, you have fought off the cancer bad guys
and helped so many animal friends. You've
stayed super positive and super happy. When
something disappoints, you smile it away, and if
something is wrong, you do your best to fix it.
You truly are SuperClara! We love you—big time."

# Author's Note

# Help Cure Child Brain Cancer

## *Message to the Kids from the Real Clara:*

No matter what goes wrong in your day, be
positive and happy. If something disappoints,
smile it away. If something is wrong,
do your best to fix it.

I do have one favor to ask. If there is a hospital
near you with sick kids, stop by and give another
kid a hug. If there isn't one nearby, find a kid
with cancer you can write to. There is one thing
I know for sure, love and kindness cures.

# Help Extend A Child's Life

## *Message to the Parents from Robert and Keira:*

Essentially all cancer research funding is focused on finding a cure. Recent advancements in DNA and RNA sequencing, immunotherapy, and vaccine technology is providing optimism. Nevertheless, a cure is likely years away.

There are several million terminal patients who wake up each day to the dark reality that a cure is not imminent. Worse, there are few, if any, options of receiving a treatment that might extend their life until there is a cure, thus wiping out any sense of hope. Hope alone offers curative properties. Add this to the possibility a *life sustaining treatment* might offer, can only have an upside.

The mission of Bridge to a Cure is to provide funding to research efforts determined to develop life-sustaining treatments. The expectation is that the research will not only consider current and prior clinical trials, but also drugs that are off patent, and many of the non-traditional treatments.

To learn more about Bridge to a Cure and to provide your support, please visit **www.BridgetoaCure.org**